The Tiara Club
at Pearl Palace

For Princess Elaine,
a wondeful editor
xxx VF

With special thanks to JD

www.tiaraclub.co.uk

ORCHARD BOOKS
338 Euston Road, London NW1 3BH
Orchard Books Australia
Level 17/207 Kent St, Sydney, NSW 2000

A Paperback Original
First published in 2007 by Orchard Books

A CIP catalogue record for this book is available from the British Library.

ISBN 978 1 84616 502 3

1 3 5 7 9 10 8 6 4 2

Printed in Great Britain

The paper and board used in this paperback are natural recyclable products made from wood grown in sustainable forests. The manufacturing processes conform to the environmental regulations of the country of origin.

Orchard Books is a division of Hachette Children's Books, an Hachette Livre UK company.

www.orchardbooks.co.uk

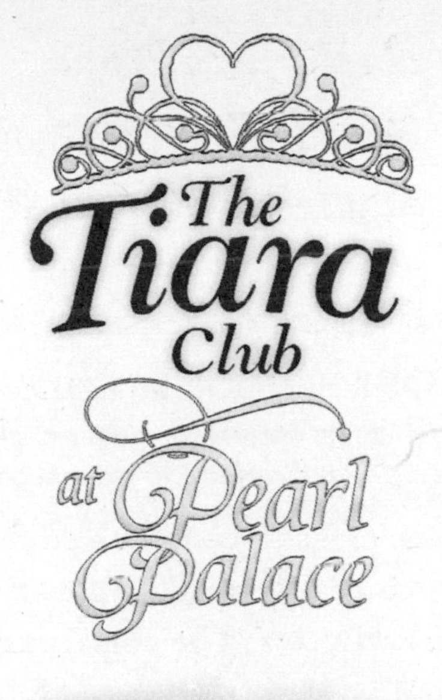

and the Enchanted Fawn

By Vivian French

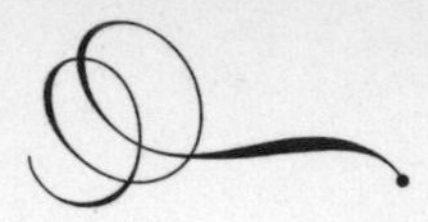

The Royal Palace Academy
for the Preparation of Perfect Princesses

(Known to our students as "*The Princess Academy*")

OUR SCHOOL MOTTO:

A Perfect Princess always thinks of others before herself, and is kind, caring and truthful.

Pearl Palace offers a complete education for Tiara Club princesses with emphasis on the arts and outdoor activities. The curriculum includes:

A special Princess Sports Day

A trip to the Magical Mountains

Preparation for the Silver Swan Award (stories and poems)

A visit to the King Rudolfo's Exhibition of Musical Instruments

Our headteacher, King Everest, is present at all times, and students are well looked after by the head fairy godmother, Fairy G, and her assistant, Fairy Angora.

Our resident staff and visiting experts include:

QUEEN MOLLY
(Sports and games)

LADY MALVEENA
(Secretary to King Everest)

LORD HENRY
(Natural History)

QUEEN MOTHER MATILDA
(Etiquette, Posture and Flower Arranging)

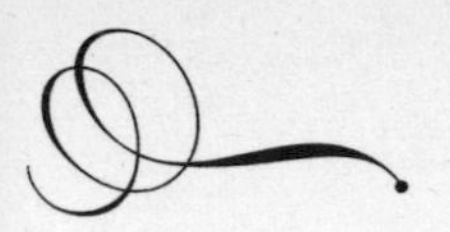

We award tiara points to encourage our Tiara Club princesses towards the next level. All princesses who win enough points at Pearl Palace will be presented with their Pearl Sashes and attend a celebration ball.

Pearl Sash Tiara Club princesses are invited to go on to Emerald Castle, our very special residence for Perfect Princesses, where they may continue their education at a higher level.

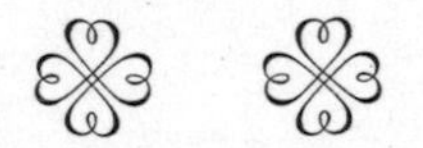

PLEASE NOTE:
Pets are not allowed at Pearl Palace.
Princesses are expected to arrive at the Academy with a *minimum* of:

TWENTY BALLGOWNS
(with all necessary hoops, petticoats, etc)

TWELVE DAY DRESSES

SEVEN GOWNS
suitable for garden parties, and other special day occasions

TWELVE TIARAS

DANCING SHOES
five pairs

VELVET SLIPPERS
three pairs

RIDING BOOTS
two pairs

Cloaks, muffs, stoles, gloves and other essential accessories as required

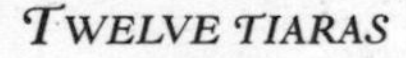

Hello, and how are you?
I'm Princess Ellie, and I'm one of the
Lily Room princesses - but you probably
know that already if you've met my friends
Hannah, Isabella, Lucy, Grace and Sarah.
I do hope you have; they're SO lovely -
just like you! We have lots of fun
when we're together - as long
as the twins aren't around...

Chapter One

Have you ever seen a little fawn? I hadn't – not until we went to help Witch Windlespin. She'd found the fawn wandering all by itself in Hollyberry Wood after a dreadful storm, and she was worried because she couldn't find the poor little thing's mother. She sent a message to Fairy G (that's our school fairy godmother) to ask her for help, and Fairy G decided we could ALL help...and of course we were thrilled to bits!

Oh – perhaps I should tell you about Witch Windlespin. She's not one of those horrid witches who ride on broomsticks, or make scary spells. She weaves the most beautiful material, and makes fabulous clothes, and magic herbal medicines as well. We met her when we were in Silver Towers, and she was SO amazing! But when we climbed out of our coaches outside her cottage in Hollyberry Wood, she was standing waiting for us and looking really worried.

"I don't understand it," she told Fairy G. "I've lived here for years and years, and I know Velvet Ear well, and she's a wonderful mother.

She'd never abandon her baby – but where is she? I thought she'd come here as soon as she realised he was lost, but there's been no sign of her. I've tried to look for her, but her little one has been very miserable, and I can't leave him for long."

Fairy G smiled one of her huge beaming smiles. "I've got all the Pearl Palace princesses here to help," she said. "I'm certain we'll find Velvet Ear before the end of the day."

Witch Windlespin looked delighted. "That's so kind." She turned to us. "Would you like to see Velvet Ear's baby? I've given him a herbal drink, so he's asleep, but you could have a little peep at him."

"Won't we wake him up?" I asked.

Witch Windlespin shook her head. "It's an enchanted sleep. I'll wake him when his mother is safely back beside him."

We were SO excited! Fairy G made us get into line, and we tiptoed round the back of Witch Windlespin's cottage to a pretty

little summerhouse. The fawn was tucked up in a wicker basket lined with the softest green moss, and he looked absolutely adorable. He had the longest eyelashes, but every so often he gave a tiny sigh as if he was missing his mother even in his sleep.

"We HAVE to find Velvet Ear," Grace said as we walked away.

Diamonde, who was behind us, snorted. "It's only a deer," she sneered. "It's not as if it was something important. I don't know why everyone's making such a fuss!"

Gruella shook her head. "But he's SO gorgeous!"

Gruella doesn't often disagree with Diamonde, and we looked at her in surprise.

Diamonde tossed her blonde curls. "You go and find the fluffy wuffy deer then, Gruella. I'M going to pick a huge bunch of flowers!" And before anyone could stop her she sailed off into Hollyberry Wood, her nose in the air.

Gruella looked after her anxiously. "Oh dear," she said. "Maybe I'd better go with her...she'll be furious with me if I don't."

"You can come with us, if you like." Lucy's always very kind. "You'd be very welcome."

"I'd better go after her," Gruella said, and she hurried off in the direction Diamonde had gone.

Chapter Two

Not long after Gruella had disappeared, Fairy G came stomping round the corner.

"Where's Gruella?" she asked Hannah. "And Diamonde?"

Hannah's much too nice to tell tales. "They...they've already gone into Hollyberry Wood," she said.

"Hm." Fairy G didn't look very

pleased. "They should have waited to be told what to do. Still, I don't suppose they'll go very far, and they'll be together. Now, I want the rest of you to keep in groups. I'm going to give each group a bag of coloured pebbles so you can mark which way you walk. If you see Velvet Ear don't frighten her; just hurry back here as quickly as you can, leaving the pebbles to show Witch Windlespin where she is."

"What if we don't find her?" Isabella asked.

"Then you pick up your pebbles as you make your way back. And remember – if you run out of pebbles, DON'T go any further. Turn round at once. Is everyone quite clear what to do?"

We all nodded, but then Grace asked, "Are there any other deer? How will we know which one is Velvet Ear?"

Witch Windlespin smiled. "That's a very sensible question. You'll know her at once, because one of her ears is bigger than the other."

"Well done, Grace." Fairy G handed her a string bag full of

pebbles, and waved her wand. There was a fizzling noise, and the pebbles turned bright blue. "There you are! Each group will have its own colour so you don't get muddled. Off you go, Lily Room – and good luck!"

Hollyberry Wood was SO pretty. There were lots of wild flowers everywhere, and the trees were covered in blossom. Birds were hopping about from branch to branch, singing as if they were trying to win the birdsong of the year competition. Of course I was with all my friends from Lily Room, and if we hadn't been worried about Velvet Ear we'd have enjoyed every second. We looked this way and that as we walked along, dropping pebbles whenever our path divided, but there was no sign of her...and then we came to this very very tall beech tree.

Now, I don't know if you've got any brothers and sisters, but I have – and when I'm at home we spend a lot of time playing in our palace gardens. And I do hope you won't think I'm very unprincessy, but I just LOVE climbing trees. It's not something I tell my mum and dad about (I just KNOW they'd say Perfect Princesses NEVER climb trees!) but it's such fun! And when I saw the beech tree an idea popped into my head.

"Supposing we climbed to the top?" I suggested. "If we did, I'm sure we'd be able to see right over the wood – and we could see where Velvet Ear is!"

Lucy looked at me doubtfully. "I'm not very good at climbing up trees."

"Nor me," Isabella agreed. "Supposing we fell off? We'd be no help finding Velvet Ear then."

"I think it'll be OK if we're careful," Hannah said. "Ellie's right – we would be able to see for miles. Why don't Ellie and I climb up, and the rest of you can watch from down below?"

Sarah, Lucy and Isabella nodded, but Grace stepped forward. "I'm going to climb as well," she announced.

I looked round, but there was no sign of Fairy G or any of the other Pearl Palace princesses. I couldn't help feeling relieved; no one had told us we were forbidden to climb trees, but I still felt as if we might be doing something wrong.

"Here I go!" I called, and I tucked up my dress and swung myself into the lowest branches. Grace and Hannah followed behind me, and to begin with it was as easy as going upstairs.

Up and up we went, until gradually the branches grew thinner.

"Ooooh," Hannah said. "It's a bit wobbly up here..."

"I don't think we should go any higher." Grace was holding on so tightly her knuckles were white. "My brother says it's stupid to take risks."

"I'll just go up to that branch there," I said, "and then I'll be higher than all the other trees..."

And I was right. It was so AMAZING! I felt like a bird as I looked down on Hollyberry

Wood. Witch Windlespin's cottage looked like a doll's house, and I could see Pearl Palace princesses scattered all over the different paths. Then I saw a tiny movement in the middle of a thick clump of bushes, and I screwed up my eyes and stared…

Chapter Three

It was Velvet Ear. I was almost certain, although I was too high up to be able to see if one ear was bigger than the other. She was lying half hidden by leaves and flowers...and there was a little fawn beside her!

"Hannah," I called down, "Grace – can you see where I'm pointing?

Can you see those bushes...the ones covered in white flowers?"

There was a rustling as my friends peered through the leaves, and then Hannah said, "Yes! I can see them. Why?"

"I think Velvet Ear's in the middle, and there's another fawn with her!" I told her. "She's lying down – I can't tell if she's asleep, or if something is wrong. We've got to tell Witch Windlespin how to find them...I don't think anyone could see them, even if they were really close."

"Could we mark the way with our pebbles?" Grace asked.

"We could try," I said as I began to climb down, "if we've got enough. Come on – let's go and see!"

Back at the bottom of the tree, Isabella picked up the bag of pebbles. "There aren't many left," she said. "What should we do?"

We looked at each other for a moment, and then Sarah said, "Why don't we make an arrow?"

"Brilliant!" Hannah patted her on the back, and she and Sarah arranged the last blue pebbles so they pointed straight towards the bushes where Velvet Ear was lying. Then we hurried off, and we were SO glad we had the pebbles to follow – it's amazing how difficult it is to remember the way when all the trees and bushes and little twisty paths look exactly the same! Even with the pebbles to show us which path to take we did hesitate a couple of times, especially when we saw a sweet little stream that none of us remembered.

"I'm sure we didn't see that before!" Isabella said as we stopped to stare at it.

"We were coming from the other direction," Grace pointed out. "Maybe it was hidden by those reeds?"

There was a sudden sound of a giggle, and we whirled round – but there was no sign of anyone.

"Did you hear that?" Lucy asked nervously. "Who could it be?"

"We haven't got time to look," I said. "Come on – we've really got to get back. Look – there's a blue pebble over there! That MUST be the path!"

But after we'd rushed along the path for what felt like ages and ages we didn't find even one blue pebble...and then the path divided, and we had absolutely no idea whether we should go left or right. Hannah, Lucy and I went a little way up one path, and Isabella, Sarah and Grace went up the other...and there was nothing to show the way. We met back at the place where the path divided.

"I think," Isabella said slowly, "we're lost."

Chapter Four

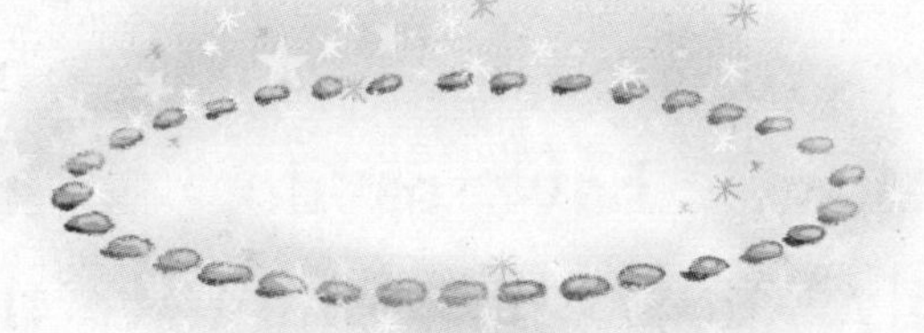

I'm not really brave. When Isabella said we were lost I could feel butterflies in my stomach, but I SO don't like giving up on anything. Also, I couldn't help thinking about that nasty little giggle. Someone had been playing games with us...and I was almost certain I knew who it was.

I didn't tell my friends, though. I told myself "A Perfect Princess always thinks the best of others," and concentrated on trying to cheer everyone up.

"All we have to do," I said firmly, "is go back until we find the stream again. Once we're there we can follow the trail back to the tall tree, and then we'll know where we are."

"But we still won't know the way out of Hollyberry Wood." Lucy's voice was wobbly, and I saw Sarah move closer to her and squeeze her hand.

"No," I said, "but I can climb

up high again, and see which way we should go. And if the worst comes to the worst perhaps we can signal from the tree."

"Wow!" Grace grinned at me. "Any minute now you'll be killing dragons, Ellie!"

"What dragons?" Sarah's eyes widened.

"I was only joking," Grace told her. "Come on – let's get going."

We held hands as we hurried back, and we found the stream quite quickly.

"Now to look for our trail." Lucy sounded much more cheerful, and a moment later she said, "Look! There they are—OH!"

We stood in a row and stared. Someone had collected up loads of our blue pebbles and arranged them in a circle...so there was no trail at all.

"What do we do now?" Isabella asked, and I realised all my friends were looking at me as if I might know the answer.

"Right from when we left the cottage," I said slowly, "the sun was on our backs. If we take that path over there, the sun will be behind us..." My heart was pitter-pattering in an anxious sort of way, and I SO hoped I wasn't going to get Lily Room even more lost. "What do you think?"

"I think that sounds really clever," Grace said. "Does everyone agree we go that way?"

Hannah, Isabella, Lucy and Sarah nodded.

"Let's go!" Grace picked up a stick, and waved it as we set off yet again. And we hadn't been walking for more than about five minutes when we saw the beech tree right in front of us.

"Hurrah!" I said. I'd been getting really, really worried, although I'd tried not to show it.

"Sh!" Sarah held up a finger. We stopped to listen – and heard the sound of someone crying their eyes out. We hurried round to the other side of the tree, and there were Diamonde and Gruella.

They were curled up in a heap like the babes in the wood, and Gruella's face was bright red, and Diamonde's was streaked with tears. When they saw us they struggled to their feet and ran towards us – and Gruella hugged Hannah, and Diamonde actually hugged me! I hugged her back and patted her shoulders, and I tried SO hard not to let her see how surprised I was.

"We thought we'd be here for ever and ever," Gruella sobbed. "We walked round and round and ROUND, and at first it was fun because we picked some pretty flowers. Then we found all these blue pebbles, and Diamonde said someone must be playing a silly game so we moved them...but then we didn't know which way to go back to the cottage... Ooooooooooooh!" And she began to cry again, but much more quietly.

Diamonde straightened herself, moved quickly away, and blew her nose.

"You didn't have to tell them everything I said, Gruella," she said crossly. She turned to me, but I didn't wait to hear what she had to say.

"Shhh..." I whispered, and pointed.

For a moment every single one of us stood as still as if we were frozen. Even Gruella stopped sniffing as the most beautiful deer stepped cautiously out from the green leaves.

She looked at us with her big brown eyes, and we held our breath. Slowly she came a little closer, and then – and it was SO hard not to gasp with excitement – a tiny fawn came slowly limping after her.

Chapter Five

I knew at once the deer was Velvet Ear. One of her ears was definitely bigger than the other, but also there was something in the way she looked at us that made me sure she was used to humans. She looked straight at me, and then she did the most amazing thing. She bent her head, and pushed the fawn towards me. Hardly daring to breathe, I bent down, and again Velvet Ear nudged the fawn almost into my arms. Very VERY gently I picked him up, watching Velvet Ear all the time to make sure this was what she wanted. And then, as I cradled him, she actually nodded...and then began walking down the path in the most determined way. When we didn't follow at once she stopped and looked over her shoulder, and you could SO see she was thinking, "Silly humans!" We tiptoed after her, and she went on walking. I could hardly believe what was happening. I was carrying a real live fawn, and following its mother...it was completely magic!

As we came near the edge of the wood Velvet Ear began to look worried, and I could tell why. There was SUCH a babbling of anxious voices, and I could hear Fairy G booming, "If they're not back in five minutes I think we should send out a search party!"

"Oh dear," I whispered to Sarah, who was walking beside me. "Could you run on ahead, and tell them to be quiet?"

Sarah nodded, and as Velvet Ear drew back into the shelter of the trees she ran past and out into the sunshine. I was half expecting a cheer, but instead I heard Fairy G bellow, "Aha! Here come the Lily Room princesses! Sarah dear, have you see Diamonde and Gruella? We're very worried about them!"

I didn't hear what Sarah said in reply, but she must have hushed everyone, because all of a sudden the voices went quiet.

A moment later Witch Windlespin came hurrying towards us. Velvet Ear gave the softest sigh, as if she just knew everything was going to be all right, and Witch Windlespin held out her arms to her.

"DEAR Velvet Ear," she said as she stroked the deer's soft neck, "where have you been? Your baby's quite safe..." And then she saw the fawn that I was carrying, and her eyes shone.

"That's why Velvet Ear couldn't come and find you," I said. "This is her other fawn – and he's hurt his leg." I was going to give the poor little thing to Witch Windlespin, but Velvet Ear moved between us.

"She trusts you," the witch told me. "You carry him to the cottage...take him round to the summerhouse at the back."

It was fantastic! We came out of the wood in a procession, and Fairy G and all the Pearl Palace princesses stood and watched us. Witch Windlespin led the way

with her arm round Velvet Ear's neck, and then I followed with the fawn. Behind me came all my friends...and finally Diamonde and Gruella trailed at the rear, looking SO sorry for themselves.

We never told Fairy G what happened in Hollyberry Wood (Perfect Princesses NEVER tell tales), but I think she must have guessed at least a little bit of what had happened. She told the twins off for running into the woods before she had given out proper instructions, and she wouldn't let them come round to the summerhouse to see what happened when Velvet Ear found her lost baby. Of course we watched it all, and it was SO sweet! Fairy G waved her wand, and just one golden star floated down onto the sleeping fawn's head...and he sneezed, and woke up – and then he absolutely LEAPT out of the basket and danced round and round Velvet Ear.

Then the star floated off, and landed on the fawn in my arms...and when I put him down on the grass, his limp was completely gone! He ran towards his brother, and the two of them rubbed noses before skipping back to Velvet Ear's side.

"Thank you, my dear, dear princesses," Witch Windlespin said, and she smiled at us. "You did very well today."

"Quite right!" Fairy G beamed happily. "I think Lily Room deserve at least ten tiara points each, don't you, Witch Windlespin?"

"What about us?" said a whining voice, and Diamonde pushed her way forward. "Gruella and I came back with the deer as well. Why aren't we getting points too?"

Fairy G didn't answer, but Witch

Windlespin began to laugh. It took me a second to see why, but then I realised – Velvet Ear was shaking her head!

Diamonde went bright red, grabbed Gruella's arm, and disappeared.

"I think it's time to let Velvet Ear and her babies make their way back to Hollyberry Wood," Witch Windlespin said. "But perhaps all you wonderful Pearl Palace princesses would like to join me in a picnic here in my garden?"

Chapter Six

The picnic was GLORIOUS. Fairy G waved her wand again and again, and at once the ground was covered in pretty pink satin cushions. A table sprang up from nowhere, and so did a lemonade fountain – and then Witch Windlespin brought plate after plate of the most delicious sandwiches and cakes out of her cottage. Twelve of the sweetest birds you ever saw flew down onto a twig, and began to sing for us – it was SO amazing!

After we'd eaten, we sat on the cushions and Witch Windlespin told us fabulous stories about all the animals that lived in Hollyberry Wood. It was one of the loveliest afternoons you could ever imagine...

And when we were in the coach rolling steadily home, I looked round at my very special friends, and I thought how lucky I was...

And do you know what makes it even MORE special?

You're my friend too!

What happens next?
Find out in
Princess Sarah
and the Silver Swan

Hello! I'm Princess Sarah!

Do you ever get into a panic about things at the last minute? I do! When I realised it was almost the end of term, I went hot and cold. Luckily my friends from Lily Room are very good at calming me down. I don't know what I'd do without Hannah, Isabella, Lucy, Grace and Ellie...and you.

Look out for

Princess Parade

with Princess Hannah and Princess Lucy

ISBN 978 1 84616 504 7

And look out for the Daffodil Room princesses in the Tiara Club at Emerald Castle:

Princess Amelia and the Silver Seal
Princess Leah and the Golden Seahorse
Princess Ruby and the Enchanted Whale
Princess Millie and the Magical Mermaid
Princess Rachel and the Dancing Dolphin
Princess Zoe and the Wishing Shell

Win a Tiara Club Perfect Princess Prize!

Look for the secret word in mirror writing that is hidden in a tiara in each of the Tiara Club books. Each book has one word. Put together the six words from books 19 to 24 to make a special Perfect Princess sentence, then send it to us together with 20 words or more on why you like the Tiara Club books. Each month, we will put the correct entries in a draw and one lucky reader will receive a magical Perfect Princess prize!

Send your Perfect Princess sentence,
at least 20 words on why you like the Tiara Club,
your name and your address on a postcard to:
THE TIARA CLUB COMPETITION,
Orchard Books, 338 Euston Road,
London, NW1 3BH

Australian readers should write to:
Hachette Children's Books,
Level 17/207 Kent Street, Sydney, NSW 2000.

Only one entry per child.
Final draw: 30 September 2008

By Vivian French
Illustrated by Sarah Gibb

The Tiara Club

PRINCESS CHARLOTTE AND THE BIRTHDAY BALL	ISBN	978 1 84362 863 7
PRINCESS KATIE AND THE SILVER PONY	ISBN	978 1 84362 860 6
PRINCESS DAISY AND THE DAZZLING DRAGON	ISBN	978 1 84362 864 4
PRINCESS ALICE AND THE MAGICAL MIRROR	ISBN	978 1 84362 861 3
PRINCESS SOPHIA AND THE SPARKLING SURPRISE	ISBN	978 1 84362 862 0
PRINCESS EMILY AND THE BEAUTIFUL FAIRY	ISBN	978 1 84362 859 0

The Tiara Club at Silver Towers

PRINCESS CHARLOTTE AND THE ENCHANTED ROSE	ISBN	978 1 84616 195 7
PRINCESS KATIE AND THE DANCING BROOM	ISBN	978 1 84616 196 4
PRINCESS DAISY AND THE MAGICAL MERRY-GO-ROUND	ISBN	978 1 84616 197 1
PRINCESS ALICE AND THE CRYSTAL SLIPPER	ISBN	978 1 84616 198 8
PRINCESS SOPHIA AND THE PRINCE'S PARTY	ISBN	978 1 84616 199 5
PRINCESS EMILY AND THE WISHING STAR	ISBN	978 1 84616 200 8

The Tiara Club at Ruby Mansions

PRINCESS CHLOE AND THE PRIMROSE PETTICOATS	ISBN	978 1 84616 290 9
PRINCESS JESSICA AND THE BEST-FRIEND BRACELET	ISBN	978 1 84616 291 6
PRINCESS GEORGIA AND THE SHIMMERING PEARL	ISBN	978 1 84616 292 3
PRINCESS OLIVIA AND THE VELVET CLOAK	ISBN	978 1 84616 293 0
PRINCESS LAUREN AND THE DIAMOND NECKLACE	ISBN	978 1 84616 294 7
PRINCESS AMY AND THE GOLDEN COACH	ISBN	978 1 84616 295 4

The Tiara Club at Pearl Palace

PRINCESS HANNAH AND THE LITTLE BLACK KITTEN	ISBN	978 1 84616 498 9
PRINCESS ISABELLA AND THE SNOW-WHITE UNICORN	ISBN	978 1 84616 499 6
PRINCESS LUCY AND THE PRECIOUS PUPPY	ISBN	978 1 84616 500 9
PRINCESS GRACE AND THE GOLDEN NIGHTINGALE	ISBN	978 1 84616 501 6
PRINCESS ELLIE AND THE ENCHANTED FAWN	ISBN	978 1 84616 502 3
PRINCESS SARAH AND THE SILVER SWAN	ISBN	978 1 84616 503 0
BUTTERFLY BALL	ISBN	978 1 84616 470 5
CHRISTMAS WONDERLAND	ISBN	978 1 84616 296 1
PRINCESS PARADE	ISBN	978 1 84616 504 7

All priced at £3.99.
Butterfly Ball, Christmas Wonderland and *Princess Parade* are priced at £5.99.
The Tiara Club books are available from all good bookshops, or can be ordered direct from the publisher: Orchard Books, PO BOX 29, Douglas IM99 IBQ.
Credit card orders please telephone 01624 836000
or fax 01624 837033 or visit our website: www.orchardbooks.co.uk
or e-mail: bookshop@enterprise.net for details.

To order please quote title, author and ISBN and your full name and address.
Cheques and postal orders should be made payable to 'Bookpost plc.'
Postage and packing is FREE within the UK
(overseas customers should add £2.00 per book).

Prices and availability are subject to change.

Check out

website at:

www.tiaraclub.co.uk

You'll find Perfect Princess games and fun things to do, as well as news on the Tiara Club and all your favourite princesses!